# Balaam

The
Story
of
Glops,
Short
Story 5a

## Betty M Reeves

# *Balaam*
## *The Story of Glops, Short Story 5a*

Betty M Reeves

Copyright © 2020 Betty's Music & Publishing

**ISBN:** 979-8-9900790-7-6

Betty's Music & Publishing

155 E. Ocla Street
Borger, TX  79007
betty@txcredit.com
www.bettymreeves-author.com
www.bettyspublishing.com
Facebook.com/bettymreevesauthor


Photography: Betty M Reeves and free images online


Numbers 23:19-21 is from the Holy Bible, New International Reader's Version, Copyright © 1995, 1996, 1998, 2014 by Biblica, Inc. All rights reserved. Published by Zondervan, Grand Rapids, Michigan 49546.

The story of Balaam is found in Numbers 22-24.

# The Glops Song

Betty M Reeves

William B. Bradbury
(1816-1868)

Chorus

Im - ag-i-nar-y, prac-tic'-ly in-vis-i-ble,

Ooz - ing slow-ly, bare-ly mo - bile,

Shy, but thought-ful and help - ful Were the

play - ful, gig - gly glops. glops.

To Verses    Ending

The melody to this chorus is one you may already know: **Jesus Loves Me**.
Have fun singing!

"God is not a mere man. He cannot lie. He is not a human being. He does not change his mind. He speaks, and then He acts. He makes a promise, and then He keeps it. He has commanded me to bless Israel. He has given them his blessing and I cannot change it. I do not see any trouble coming on the people of Jacob. I do not see any suffering in Israel. The LORD their God is with them. The shout of the King is among them."

Numbers 23:19-21

(The Holy Bible, New International Reader's Version)

# Balaam

The Israelites had wandered in the wilderness for forty years. They had won many battles against other nations and countries.

They were coming into the plains and valleys of Moab east of the Jordan River. The country of Moab was where the country of Jordan is today. Israelites were preparing for the day when they would cross the Jordan River into the land God promised them, the land flowing with milk and honey.

Glops loved to be around the Israelites and their friendly sheep, goats, oxen, donkeys, and camels. Since the glops were practically invisible, they could go almost anywhere they wanted to go.

Getting anywhere took glops a long time, though. They moved by slowly oozing along. Friendly animals helped by letting the little glops "hitch a ride" or ooze onto them.

Most of the glops stayed with the Israelites' livestock. Some glops slowly oozed through grassy fields to be with animals belonging to the Moabites.

Moab had joined forces with nearby Midian, and together they had chosen the Midianite Balak to be their ruler.

The Moabites complained to King Balak about the Israelites. "There are too many of these foreigners. They are eating everything around us like an ox eats all the grass in the fields."

The glops listened to the Moabites and thought, *The Moabites must be afraid of the Israelites. God's people have won battle after battle for forty years and will continue to win, because the LORD God Almighty is with them.*

The king knew the Israelites were powerful and that their power came from their God. *How can I get rid of these people before they start a war?* he asked himself.

He thought of a plan to protect his two nations from the immigrants. He decided to hire a well-known, powerful prophet who could put a curse on Israel. This prophet was named Balaam.

The king sent messengers to Balaam, who lived in the city of Pethor near the Euphrates River. Some glops plopped themselves on the backs of the messengers' donkeys and camels. The glops wanted to go on this new adventure that would take them along the edge of the Syrian Desert.

The messengers brought money and gifts for the prophet. They also gave their king's message to him.

"The Israelite nation has come into our land. There are too many of them and they are too powerful for us. Come and put a curse on them so that we can win a battle against them and force them out of Moab. We have heard that whomever you bless will be blessed, and whomever you curse will be cursed."

That night, God told Balaam, "Do not go with these men. You are not to curse my people, because I have already blessed them."

Also, during the night, several glops oozed off the Moabites' animals and onto the only animal that the prophet owned. She was a friendly jenny, or female donkey.

The next morning, Balaam sent the men away.

One month later, princes from Moab came to Balaam's door. They offered more money, more gifts, and a new message from their king.

"Let nothing keep you from coming to us, for we will greatly honor you and make you rich. We will do whatever you ask. Please, come and curse these people for us."

These princes were important men in Moab. To impress them, the prophet said, "Even if your king would give me his palace filled with silver and gold, I could do nothing except what God commands."

Balaam did not like Israelites. He wanted to carry out King Balak's request to curse them. He thought that he himself was the only prophet who could do it. And he wanted to be rich.

Balaam was so full of pride that God decided to teach him a lesson in humility.

That night, God said, "You may go with these men, but you must only do what I tell you."

The next morning, the prophet told the princes he would go to Moab with them. He told two servants to go with him. He saddled his gentle jenny. Several glops were on the donkey. Together they began their journey.

Suddenly, the glops and the donkey saw an angel standing in the path. He was holding a sword and was ready for battle.

1622 De profeet Bileam en de ezel, Pieter Lastman (ca. 1583-1633)
Israel Museum, Jerusalem, Israel

When she saw the angel, the jenny turned off the path and went into a field.

*Oh my! We see the Angel!* The glops jiggled with excitement.

*He is the Angel of the LORD!*

They wiggled and looked around to see Him.

*Where did He go?*

Like most donkeys, the jenny liked everything to be ordinary and not strange. She needed time to think about what she wanted to do.

Balaam had seen nothing and wanted his donkey to behave. He pulled on her bridle, and he hit her.

The glops were shocked at his anger. They began to spread out over the donkey's body to protect her from Balaam's blows. He hit the jenny until she returned to the path.

Detail from 1834 Landschaft mit Bileam anagoia, Joseph Anton Koch (1768-1839)
Germanisches Nationalmuseum, Nuremberg, Bavaria, Germany

The jenny was now on alert. She and the glops kept looking for the Angel.

*Look! There! Just ahead of us!*

The Angel stood in a narrow place.

There was no room for the jenny to turn right or left.

Having no place to go, she simply lay down.

Balaam was furious and began to beat her with his stick.

The glops continued to keep the jenny from getting hurt.

1626 *Bileam en zijn ezelin*, Rembrandt Harmensz van Rijn (1606 – 1669)
Musée Cognacq-Jay, Paris, France

The Lord opened the jenny's mouth and she spoke, "What have I done to you? Why have you hit me three times?"

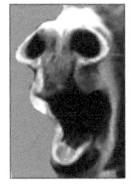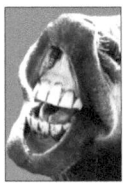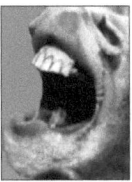

Balaam answered the jenny as if talking with the donkey was a normal thing to do. "You have made me look foolish in front of the Moabite princes. I wish I had a sword in my hand. If I did, I would kill you right now."

"I am the donkey that you have always ridden all of your life. Have I ever behaved badly before now?"

"No."

The LORD allowed Balaam's eyes to see that the Angel of the LORD with a sword in his hand was standing in the path.

The prophet immediately got off his donkey and bowed down with his face all the way to the ground.

"Why have you beaten your donkey?" the Angel asked. "I have come to stop you because what you plan to do is evil. Your donkey saw Me and stayed away from Me three times. If she had not stayed away from Me, I would have killed you with my sword and let her live."

"I have been wrong," Balaam said. "I had no idea You were here and that You wanted to stop me. If You are not pleased with me, I will go back to Pethor."

"I am not pleased with you, but you will go to Moab with the princes. You will only be able to say exactly what I give you to say. You will only be able to do exactly what I want you to do."

After that, Balaam, the jenny, and the glops no longer saw the Angel. They went with the princes.

The princes had watched Balaam. They thought he was acting crazy. First, he beat his donkey and yelled at her. Then, he got off his donkey and bowed to the ground, as if he were worshiping the beast. The men wondered if all prophets acted as nutty as this one.

The glops were sad that the princes did not believe in Almighty God and had not been able to see the Angel of the LORD.

When King Balak met them at the border of Moab, Balaam said, "I have come to you, but I can only speak the words that God puts in my mouth."

# 16

Early the next morning, the king and the princes took Balaam to a mountain where they could see the Israelite camp. The glops on the jenny could see God's people going about their daily lives.

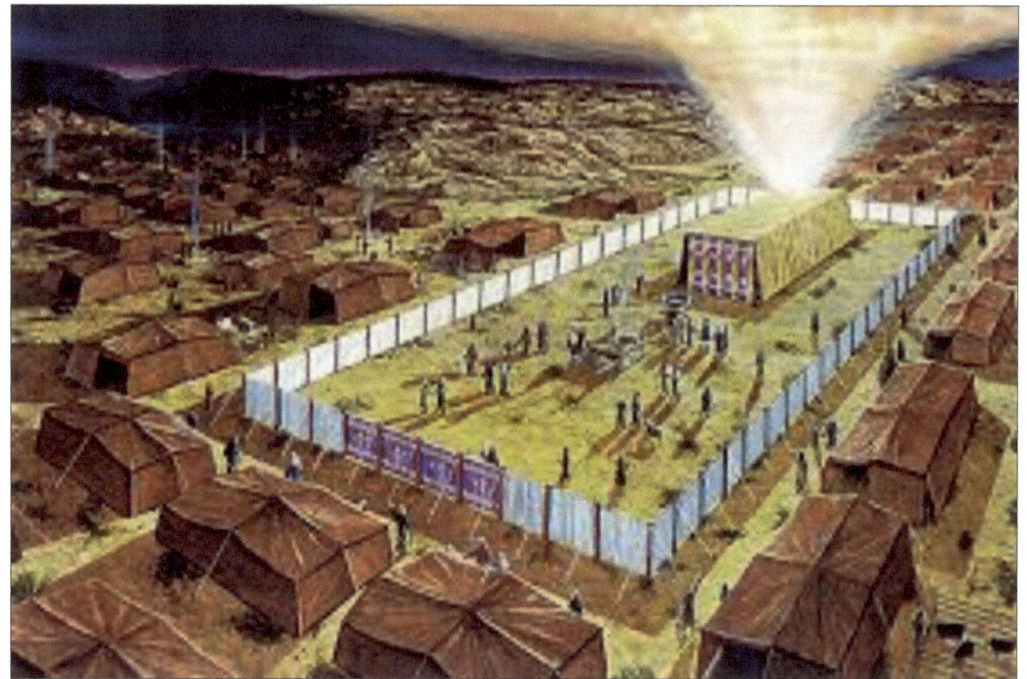

The prophet told the king to build seven altars to offer sacrifices to God. The LORD put a message in Balaam's mouth. Instead of curses, he spoke wonderful blessings and praises.

The king was very unhappy. "What have you done to me? I brought you here to curse my enemies. Instead, you have blessed them!"

He took Balaam to another mountain in the hope that this time the prophet would speak curses. They could see the campers in the valleys and plains below. The glops could see other glops and friendly animals.

"God never lies. When He makes a promise, He keeps it," Balaam said. "He has given Israel His blessing and has commanded me to bless them, too. I cannot change it. I see no trouble for Israel. The LORD their God is with them, and they rejoice for the King who is among them."

"Oh, shut up," King Balak mumbled.

Once more, the king and the princes took Balaam to a mountain overlooking the Israelites.

The glops thought, *What a wonderful view of all God's people! Look! They are arranged in camps, tribe by tribe.*

As if he heard the glops, Balaam blessed all the tribes of Israel.

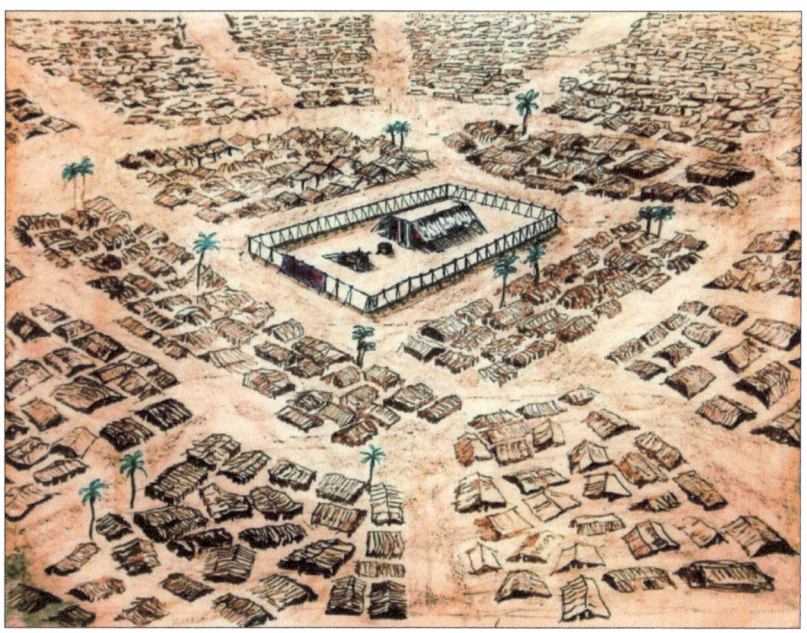

King Balak was burning with anger. "I brought you here to curse my enemies. You blessed them three times. I could have made you a very rich man living in your own palace. Your God has kept you poor. Get away from here. Take your ugly little donkey and go back to your ugly little house."

As Balaam was leaving, he turned to the king and forewarned that the Israelites would win all battles with the Moabites and their neighbors.

He predicted the future, saying, "I see Him, but not now. I see Him, but He isn't near. A star will come from the people of Jacob, and a King will rise up from Israel. One who comes from among the people of Jacob will rule."

The glops knew that the beautiful words were God's truth.

Balaam said exactly what God told him about the time our Messiah would come and save all the people who believe in Him. His prophecy is one of hundreds in the Old Testament of the Bible that are fulfilled in the life, death, and resurrection of Jesus Christ. Balaam's prophecy and many others will be completed when Jesus Christ returns again.

## About the Author

**Betty M Reeves** has written two music books, *Melody Street: Story and Illustrations* and *Guitars & Folk Songs: An Anthology*. The first was listed in the internationally recognized catalog, Kodaly-Related Publications. *The Story of Glops*, a Christian historical fiction series of nine books and two short stories for children, middle grades, and young adults. One of her books debuted at #1 New Release in Noah's Ark Stories on Kindle, and another debuted at #1 Teen and Young Adult Christian Bible Stories on Amazon. Two others were nominated for the Christian Indie Awards. Betty is an author, producer, self-publisher, arranger/composer, church musician, and  retired music teacher. Betty's Music & Publishing is her company. She is a member of Christian Indie Books, Texas High Plains Writers Association, Word Weavers Critique Group, Literary Ladies Book Club, and First Baptist Church of Amarillo. Betty holds degrees from WTA&M and TTU. She and her husband, Glenn, live in Borger and Amarillo. They are blessed with five children, nine grandchildren, many great-grandchildren, and an adorable Yorkie.

## About the "Glops" Creator

**Elayne M Hoover-Sims** enjoys storytelling, martial arts, and all kinds of creative crafts, especially Hittie dolls and doll houses. She is a project manager for Catapult systems, an IT outsourcing company. Her studies included coursework at Metropolitan State College of Denver and Angelo State University. Elayne and her husband Don are actively involved with the Kingdom of Ansteorra in the Society for Creative Anachronism, an international community learning about the arts, skills, and culture of the  Medieval and Renaissance Eras. Elayne and Don currently live in Austin, Texas, with several adorable pets.

Many have asked how the idea of the glops came about. Elayne's older sister needed help with a college assignment. Elayne, 14 years old at the time, helped her sister by quickly writing a short story about a funny, inquisitive little creature. About twenty-five years later, Elayne's mother, Betty, was looking in some files and found the short story. Betty had an idea, but what would Elayne think? "Go for it, Mom," she said. That was when Betty expanded the story and published it.

**Thank you for reading!**

My books are self-published and
depend heavily on word-of-mouth for promotion.

When you like what you read,
**please give reviews**

at your favorite online store, such as
Amazon.com
or Audible.com

You may also choose to **leave reviews** on
Goodreads.com
and IndieBound.org

**Thank you for reviewing!**

To keep up with future writings,
please visit:

bettymreeves-author.com
bettyspublishing.com
amazon.com/author/bettymreeves

and my blog:
bettymreeves-author.com/bettys-blog

Also, I invite you to visit, like, or follow me on

facebook.com/bettymreevesauthor
Instagram.com/bettymreeves1
"X" (Twitter)@bettymreeves1

*The Story of Glops* series includes these books:

   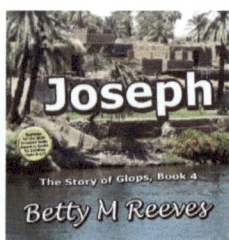

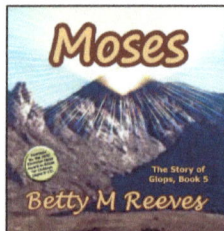  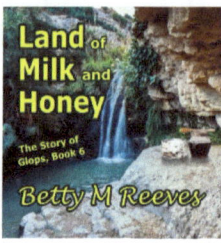 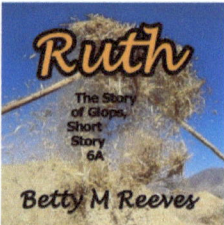

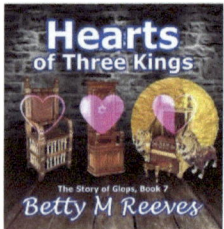 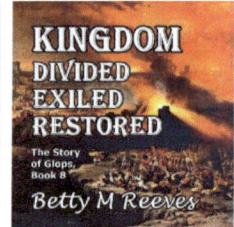 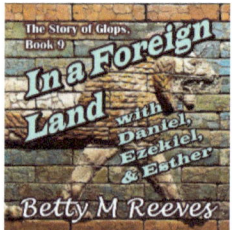

Music Books by Betty M Reeves include:

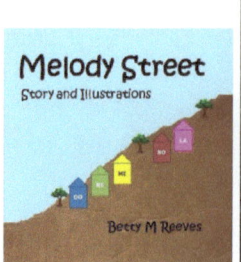 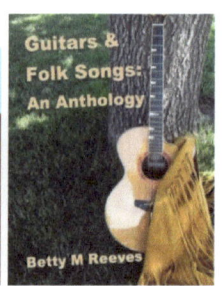

www.ingramcontent.com/pod-product-compliance
Lightning Source LLC
Chambersburg PA
CBHW041008170626
46815CB00002B/214